Karen's Stepmother

Look for these
and other books about Karen
in the
Baby-sitters Little Sister series:

Little Sister

Karen's Stepmother
Ann M. Martin

Illustrations by Susan Tang

A
LITTLE APPLE
PAPERBACK

SCHOLASTIC INC.
New York Toronto London Auckland Sydney

ISBN 0-590-47047-7

Copyright © 1994 by Ann M. Martin. All rights reserved. Published by Scholastic Inc. APPLE PAPERBACKS ® and BABY-SITTERS LITTLE SISTER ® are registered trademarks of Scholastic Inc.

12 11 10 9 8 7 6 5 4   5 6 7 8/9

Printed in the U.S.A.   40

First Scholastic printing, May 1994

*This book is in honor
of my newest cousin Alyssa Suzanne Craft.*

Welcome!

Elizabeth's Bedtime Story

"Now, Emily, what you have to remember is that this is going to be your home for a month. A whole month. Things might be a little different. But I will be around. I will take care of you like I always do."

Hello, it's me again. Karen Brewer. I was just talking to my rat, Emily Junior. We are here at Daddy's house for a month. My little brother Andrew is here too. Also Bob, his hermit crab. I am seven, and Andrew is four going on five. We both have blond hair and blue eyes. Plus I have freckles and

I wear glasses. I even have two pairs of glasses. The blue pair is for reading. The pink pair is for the rest of the time.

Knock, knock, knock. "Karen? Can I come in?"

I returned Emily Junior to her cage. Then I looked up. My big stepsister Kristy was at the door. Kristy is thirteen. I just love her. She is a gigundoly wonderful baby-sitter. Also, she is lots of fun, she is a good person to talk to, and she will always keep a secret.

"Sure," I said.

"So how are you doing?" Kristy asked me. "I cannot believe you are here for a whole month. Are you nervous?"

"Who me? No. Not at all. Andrew and I wanted to spend more time at the big house. Remember?"

"I know," replied Kristy. "Just wondering." She glanced around my room. "How is the unpacking coming along?"

"Fine. I am almost finished. I do not

2

really have much to unpack. Just this school stuff — oh! Oh, no!"

"What?" asked Kristy. "What is wrong?"

"My worksheet! Ms. Colman gave us a worksheet today. We have to finish it and hand it in tomorrow. I bet I left it at Mommy's house. I — oh, wait. Never mind. Here it is." I found the paper stuck inside a book I was reading. Whew. "I guess I have everything I need here after all," I said to Kristy. "Will you help me with this, please?"

Kristy and I worked on my sheet. Just as we were finishing it, Daddy came into the room. "Almost time for bed, pumpkin," he said.

"Okay. Daddy? Can we read together?" I asked.

"Sure. Put your pajamas on and brush your teeth. You choose the book. Then I will come back and we'll read."

The book I chose was *Howliday Inn* by Mr. James Howe. The books by Mr. James

Howe are almost always scary but funny. Daddy and I took turns reading the first chapter aloud. When we finished it, Daddy closed the book and said in a mysterious voice, "To beeee continuuuued."

I giggled. "You are silly, Daddy."

Daddy kissed me good night. Then Elizabeth came into the room. She sat on the edge of my bed and smiled at me. Elizabeth is my stepmother. Also, she is Kristy's mother. "How about a bedtime story?" she asked me.

"Daddy and I just started one," I told her.

"No," said Elizabeth. "I mean a made-up story. A story made up by me. I could tell you a little bit every night while you are here this month. I just started one for Andrew. His is about a chipmunk named Dallas."

I laughed. "What would mine be about?"

"A magic acorn," Elizabeth replied. "An acorn named Hoover who lives in Central Park in the middle of New York City."

"What makes Hoover magic?" I asked.

"Well," said Elizabeth. And she began her story. When she reached a stopping place she said, "I am so glad you and Andrew will be spending more time with us, honey."

I was pretty glad myself.

Karen's Two Mothers

In case you were wondering, Andrew and I do not live at just one home with one family like a lot of kids do. We live at two homes with two families. But we have not always done that. A long time ago, when we were much younger, we did have just one home and one family. Mommy and Daddy and Andrew and I lived here in this big house where Daddy grew up. I thought we were happy, but I guess we were not. At least, Mommy and Daddy were not. They began to fight all the time. Finally they decided to get a divorce. They did not love each other anymore (but they still loved Andrew and me). Daddy stayed in his big house, and Mommy moved into a little house. Andrew and I went with her. We lived with Daddy every other weekend. The rest of the time we lived with Mommy.

After awhile, something interesting happened. Mommy and Daddy got married again, but not to each other. Mommy married a man named Seth. Now he is our stepfather. And Daddy married Elizabeth, our stepmother. That is how Andrew and I wound up with our two families.

This is our little-house family: Mommy, Seth, Andrew, me, Rocky, Midgie, Emily Junior, and Bob. (Rocky and Midgie are Seth's cat and dog.)

This is my big-house family: Daddy, Elizabeth, Kristy, Charlie, Sam, David Michael, Emily Michelle, ˉNannie, Andrew, me, Shannon, Boo-Boo, Goldfishie, Crystal Light, Emily Junior, and Bob. Kristy, Charlie, Sam, and David Michael are Elizabeth's kids. (She was married once before she married Daddy.) So they are my stepsister and stepbrothers. Charlie and Sam are old. They go to high school. David Michael is seven like me, but he does not go to my school. (I already told you about Kristy.) Emily Michelle is my adopted sister. Daddy and Elizabeth adopted her from the faraway country of Vietnam. She is two and a half. I named my rat after her. Nannie is Elizabeth's mother (which makes her my step-grandmother). She moved in to help run the house and to help take care of all the pets and us kids. The pets are Shannon (David Michael's puppy), Boo-Boo (Daddy's fat old cat), Goldfishie and Crystal Light (can you guess what they are?), and Emily Junior and Bob. (They go back and forth between the big house and the little house with Andrew and me.)

Not long ago, another interesting thing happened. Andrew and I asked for equal time at our two houses. Now we spend a month at Daddy's, then a month at Mommy's. We are soooo happy about this change. And today is the start of our very first month at the big house. To be honest, we are just the teensiest bit nervous about it. We have never spent so much time with our big-house family — or away from Mommy. But we are looking forward to it. We were hardly able to spend any time with Daddy before.

Guess what nicknames I chose for my brother and me. I call us Andrew Two-Two and Karen Two-Two. (I thought of the names after my teacher read a book to our class. It was called *Jacob Two-Two Meets the Hooded Fang*.) We are two-twos because we have two houses and two families, two mommies and two daddies, two cats and two dogs, and two of lots of other things. Since we go back and forth between our houses, we have two bicycles, one at each house. I have two stuffed cats — Moosie at the big house, and Goosie at the little house. Plus we have clothes and books and toys at each house. I even have two best friends. Hannie Papadakis lives across the street from the big house. Nancy Dawes lives next door to the little house. (We are all in Ms. Colman's second-grade class. We call ourselves the Three Musketeers.) And of course, I have those two pairs of glasses.

Now Andrew and I had become equal-time two-twos. (So had Emily Junior and Bob.) And Elizabeth was my mother for the month.

The Magic Acorn

On Wednesday morning I woke up in my room at the big house. It was the bedroom I had grown up in until the divorce. And now it would be my bedroom for a month, instead of just on weekends. That was a nice feeling.

I hopped out of bed and dressed quickly.

"Hello, everybody!" I cried as I ran into the kitchen.

My big-house family was gathering for breakfast. Some of them looked a little sleepy. Especially Sam. But even he managed to mumble, "Morning."

The ten of us squished around the table. We passed boxes of cereal back and forth. We poured glasses of juice and milk.

"Karen, honey," said Elizabeth, "don't you want some fruit with your breakfast?"

"Mmm-mm," I replied, my mouth full of cereal. (That meant, "No, thanks.")

Elizabeth checked on everyone's meals. I chomped away and listened to the big kids. They always talk about interesting things, like dates and dances and driving cars. Charlie even has his own car. It is called the Junk Bucket. Also, he and Sam have a snowblower. Big kids are so lucky.

Just wait until I am big.

My family had to hurry through breakfast. Elizabeth said we were running late. "May I suggest that we start ten minutes earlier tomorrow?" she added. Then she glanced at me. "Karen, where are your blue glasses? Why don't you wear them around your neck so they will be with you at all times?"

12

"That is all right, Elizabeth," I replied. "I know where they are. I never forget them." (Well, hardly ever.) "They get in the way when they hang around my neck." I paused. "Hey, you know what? I just thought of something. A good — "

"Honey, you are late," said Elizabeth.

"Yeah, but a good invention — I mean, for anyone who wears glasses — and that would be me, of course — "

"Karen!" cried Elizabeth. But she was smiling.

"Let me tell you about this invention."

"*Karen!*" Now Elizabeth was laughing. "Slow down. You are talking a mile a minute. And you really are late. Charlie is waiting outside for you."

I guess I do talk too much. A lot of people have told me that. And sometimes I talk too loudly. Grown-ups are always reminding me to use my indoor voice. Oh, well. I *like* to talk.

I grabbed my things and raced outside. Charlie was going to drive Hannie and her

13

big brother Linny and me to our school in the Junk Bucket. This was *so* cool. I bet no other second-graders were driven to Stoneybrook Academy by high-school guys with their own cars.

School that day was great. Ms. Colman returned our spelling quizzes. I had gotten one hundred per cent. Hannie and Nancy and I played hopscotch at recess. Also, we jumped rope. Later, Ms. Colman told me that a poem I had written was very beautiful.

After school that day, Nannie decided to bake gingerbread. She let David Michael and Andrew and Emily and me help her. We ate the gingerbread for dessert that night, and everyone in my big-house family said it was delicious. Except for Sam, who said it was ginger-licious.

At bedtime, Daddy and I read another chapter of *Howliday Inn*. Then Elizabeth peeked into my room. "Do you want to hear some more about the magic acorn?" she asked me.

"Sure!" I replied.

The night before, Elizabeth had told me that Hoover the magic acorn had been born on an oak tree in Central Park. Now she told me how he was struck by lightning, and fell to the ground. That was when he discovered his magical powers.

I decided that my mother for the month was a gigundoly wonderful storyteller.

Chores

My first day at the big house had been wonderful. I just knew the rest of the month would be wonderful, too. I thought of reading with Daddy every single night for twenty-nine more nights. And hearing twenty-nine more parts of the story about Hoover.

I sighed with happiness when I woke up in my old room on Thursday morning. I was ready for another wonderful day. So I leaped up and dressed in a hurry. When I ran downstairs for breakfast,

Elizabeth looked at me. She frowned slightly. "Honey, are you *sure* that is what you want to wear today? An orange shirt and a pink skirt? And I don't think your socks match."

I looked down at my outfit. I had not paid much attention when I put it on. But I did not feel like changing it. I did want matching socks, though. So I ran upstairs, yelling, "I will find new socks!"

"Indoor voice!" Elizabeth called back.

After breakfast that morning, Elizabeth took Andrew and me into the living room. She said we needed to have a talk. We were not running late, so we had time for one.

"Are we in trouble?" asked Andrew.

I was wondering the same thing. I did not *think* we were, but with grown-ups, you just never know.

Elizabeth smiled. "Oh, no!" she said. "Of course not. But I want to explain something to you, now that you will be spending more time here. In this house, everybody is re-sponsible for certain chores. Even Emily.

18

Every morning, Emily helps David Michael when he feeds Shannon and Boo-Boo. David Michael also takes the trash out. Charlie drives the things we can recycle to the recycling center. Kristy vacuums. Sam irons. And everyone is responsible for making their beds and keeping their rooms neat. That is how the kids earn their allowances. Now you will have chores, too. You will make your beds, keep your rooms tidy, and take care of Emily Junior and Bob. Also, Andrew, you will help Nannie with the dusting. And Karen, you will separate the things we can recycle — the glass and metal and plastic and papers — for Charlie, so they will be ready for him to drive to the center. The recycling bins are in the garage. Do you have any questions?"

I glanced at Andrew. I was surprised. At Mommy's house we help out whenever she or Seth asks us to. But we do not have assigned chores. And I did not know the people at the big house had chores.

But do you know what Andrew said

then? He said, "I *like* to dust!"

Well, for heaven's sake.

Elizabeth smiled. Then she turned to me. "Karen?" she said.

"Okay. I will do my chores." I thought they would be easy. I always take care of Emily Junior anyway. That is not a chore.

In school that day, Ms. Colman said, "Girls and boys, who knows what special day is coming soon?"

Chris shot his hand in the air. "Memorial Day," he replied.

"Before that," said Ms. Colman.

"Oh! Mother's Day!" I cried. (I forgot to raise my hand, but Ms. Colman did not seem to mind.)

"That's right," said my teacher. "And soon we will begin making cards and gifts for whomever you would like to honor."

I knew who that would be. Mommy and Elizabeth. I would have to make two of everything. I was so busy thinking about what I would make that I forgot all about Elizabeth's chores.

Go-Carts

Friday afternoon. I just love Fridays. I like school very much, but I like the weekends, too. And I was looking forward to the big-house weekend. Nothing special had been planned, but I was sure it would be fun. You never know what might happen at the big house.

Mrs. Papadakis drove Hannie and Linny and me home from school. The weather was beautiful, and we did not want to go inside. I am so happy when the weather is warm enough for no jackets and no sweat-

21

ers, and you can play outside for hours and your hands don't get cold.

Hannie and Linny and I hung around on the Papadakises' driveway. After awhile, Andrew and David Michael came over. Then my friend Melody and her older brother Bill came over. Then Maria Kilbourne, who lives next door to Hannie, came over. Finally Timmy and Scott Hsu came over.

We talked about school. (We go to lots of different ones.) The older boys circled their bicycles in the street. Melody found some chalk and drew a hopscotch game. Linny dragged some junk out of his garage and studied it.

Soon all the boys were looking at the junk. Then the girls began to look at it, too. I did not think it was very interesting. It was just some pieces of wood and some metal rods and some screws and nails. So I was glad when Maria said, "What is it good for?"

"Building stuff," replied David Michael.

22

"What kind of stuff?" asked Andrew.

"Lots of things. Inventions," said Bill.

"A doghouse," said Hannie.

"A go-cart," said Timmy.

We all turned to look at Timmy. Now that was a good idea. If we had go-carts, we could feel like real drivers.

"A go-cart," I repeated. "Cool."

"A racing car," added Linny thoughtfully.

"Hey!" cried Scott. "I bet if we look in our garages, we can find enough parts to build a go-cart."

"I bet we could find enough parts to build lots of cars," said Bill.

"And we could race them!" exclaimed David Michael. "Right down that hill." David Michael pointed to our street. Starting where we were standing, the hill slopes down, down, down, for a long way, very slowly. We like to coast our bicycles there. Racing go-carts might be even better.

"Hey, you know what?" said Melody. "I just had a *great* idea! We could *each* build a racing car. Each one of us. And then we could hold a race. A real race, with someone yelling 'GO!' and someone at the finish line and a big audience."

"We could have it on Memorial Day," added Timmy.

Everyone thought this was a terrific idea. Everyone except Andrew. Andrew tugged at my shirt. "Karen, Karen," he said. "I do not think I can build a car all by myself."

Andrew was probably right. He was the littlest kid there. So I said, "Andrew and I will build a car together." (Even though I did not know very much about go-carts.) The other kids thought this was okay. They knew why Andrew and I were going to work together.

Then Bill added, "We don't want any help, though. Do we, you guys? We want to build our cars ourselves. No grown-ups."

We agreed. No help from adults. This was not really a rule. We just wanted to see what we could do on our own.

Elizabeth's Talk

At dinnertime, Andrew and David Michael and I ran inside. I dashed upstairs to my messy room. I fed Emily Junior. I let her play on my bed for awhile. (The bed was not made, so this did not matter.) Then I put her back in her cage and dashed downstairs for dinner.

My big-house family sat around the table. We ate spaghetti and salad. I told everyone about our racing cars.

"We are going to build them by ourselves. Well, Andrew and I will work together, but that is okay. See, what we are going to do is find stuff in our garages. Old wheels and things."

Next to me, I noticed that Andrew was raising his hand.

Elizabeth called on him. "Yes, Andrew?"

"May I have another napkin, please?"

Elizabeth found a napkin for him. Then she said, "Karen, you need to give other people a chance to speak. Andrew should not have to raise his hand at the dinner table." She smiled at me.

After dinner I decided that maybe I should make a Mother's Day card for Nannie, too. After all, she is a mother. And she lives right here in the big house with me. I would make a collage card for her. But I needed to know where to find some things.

Elizabeth was talking on the telephone. "Excuse me! Excuse me!" I whispered loudly. "Elizabeth?"

Elizabeth cupped her hand over the receiver. "Yes?"

"Where is the yarn basket?"

"In the closet in the den," she replied.

Ten minutes later I had to interrupt her again. I needed to know where the food coloring was. Then I took the art materials upstairs to my bedroom. I spread newspapers on my table before I started gluing and painting. I thought Elizabeth would like the newspapers, since they would help to keep the table clean.

I had been working hard on Nannie's card when I heard Elizabeth say, "Hi, honey. May I come in?"

"Is it already time to hear about the magic acorn?" I asked.

"Not quite yet," replied Elizabeth. "I'd like for us to have a talk. Can you come sit on the bed for a few minutes, please?"

I set Nannie's card down. It had to dry anyway. Then I joined Elizabeth on my bed.

Elizabeth looked very serious. She said, "Karen, you have not been doing your chores." (Uh-oh.) "You have not made your bed, and your room is a mess."

"I put newspapers on the table before I

28

started Nannie's card," I said.

"And that was a very smart idea," replied Elizabeth. "But that is not what I meant. I see clothes all over the floor. I see books on the floor and under the bed. I see toys everywhere. Nothing is put away."

"Well . . . I always take care of Emily Junior."

"That is a start," replied Elizabeth. "But you have other chores."

"I guess I forgot to do them."

"Okay. You need to start remembering. Andrew has remembered to do his. The other kids remember to do theirs. Well, usually. And the chores are important. They are not meant to be forgotten. Understand?"

I nodded. "Yes," I said. "Sorry."

"That's all right. Why don't I help you tidy up in here before I tell you more about Hoover? Look, if you keep all of your books on the shelves . . ."

Elizabeth had a lot of tidying-up suggestions. I guess they were helpful.

The Horrible Thought

On Saturday morning, Andrew and I woke up early. We wanted to start working on our go-cart as soon as possible. The first thing we did was rummage around in the garage and look for things we could use to build our car. We found a lot of things. The best was an old (*very* old) red wagon that nobody played with anymore.

"We can use its wheels!" I exclaimed.

Each time we found something we might be able to use, we hauled it out to the driveway. Soon a nice pile of junk sat there.

"What is the lampshade for?" Kristy asked when she came by to see what we were doing. She lifted it out of the pile.

I shrugged. "You never know," I said.

"It might make a good racing helmet," spoke up Andrew.

Kristy giggled. I guess she was imagining Andrew flying down the street with a lampshade on his head.

Oh, well. I really did not know what we would use that shade for. But I figured that — somehow — we could turn all our stuff into a go-cart. Up and down the street, our friends were collecting things, too. So was David Michael, of course. He had taken a few things from the garage. But mostly he and Linny and Bill were collecting stuff from a nearby lot where a house was being built.

Andrew and I decided garage stuff was good enough for us.

After lunch, Andrew and I were ready to work on our car again. But Daddy whispered to us, "Come to the living room. Secret meeting."

Oh, boy. A secret meeting. This is who came to it: Daddy, Andrew, me, Kristy, Charlie, Sam, David Michael, and Emily Michelle. Everybody except Elizabeth and Nannie.

"Okay," began Daddy. "As you know, next Sunday is Mother's Day. What shall we do for Elizabeth and Nannie?"

"I am making stuff in school," I said. "And at home."

"Me, too," said Andrew and David Michael.

"That is fine," replied Daddy. "But I thought we would plan a special day for them. Something more than presents."

"We could fix a Mother's Day lunch," suggested Kristy.

"We could give them breakfast in bed," said Charlie.

"We could put on a show," I said.

"A show? What kind of show?" David Michael looked interested. He is going to

be a Winkie in *The Wizard of Oz* at his school soon. He has decided he likes acting. I like it, too. Also singing and dancing.

"We could sing songs and make up skits," I said.

"Cool," said David Michael. "I will help you, Karen."

"I saw a cake in a magazine," spoke up Daddy. "It looked like a merry-go-round. Maybe we could bake it for Elizabeth and Nannie."

Everyone thought this was a good idea, even though none of us knows much about baking. "If it looks funny, you can just pile on lots of frosting and decorations," said Kristy.

After we talked for awhile, Daddy divided us into teams. David Michael and I were in charge of planning the show. Daddy and Emily would bake the cake. Charlie and Andrew would fix the breakfasts in bed. And Kristy and Sam were supposed to plan the special lunch.

What a Mother's Day this was going to

be. I was glad I had already made my three Mother's Day presents. And three cards. Wait a minute. One of those presents and one of those cards were for Mommy. Uh-oh. I had just thought a horrible thought.

8

Two Mother's Days

"Karen?" said Daddy. "Is everything all right?"

Our secret meeting was over. My big-house family was leaving the room. Except for me. And except for Daddy. Daddy was staring at me. I must have had a funny look on my face.

"Well," I began. "Well, um, no. I just thought of something."

"What is it?"

"It's about Mommy. And it is a horrible thought. I know I asked for equal time with you and Mommy. I know I said I wanted to live at the big house more. But Sunday is *Mother's* Day, Daddy. And Andrew and I will be here with you and Elizabeth. Does that mean we cannot celebrate with Mommy? Not at all?"

"Hmm," said Daddy. "I had not thought about that. Well, let me see. *Next* year, May will be a little-house month."

"But I do not want to skip Mother's Day *this* year. Mommy would be sad. That is not fair."

"You can still call Mommy. And make something for her."

"But I want to *see* her. Can't Andrew and I visit her? And what about Father's Day? Father's Day will be next month when I am at the little house. Will Andrew and I be able to see *you*? And what about our birthdays? And Christmas? And — "

"Whoa, whoa, whoa. Hold on a minute," said Daddy. "Let's take this one holiday at a time. I have to admit, we had not thought about this when we worked out the new arrangements for you and Andrew. We worked things out so that this year you will be at Mommy's for Christmas, and next year you will be here. And that this year you will be here for Thanksgiving, and next year you will be at Mommy's. But I know you want to see both of your families at the holidays. And Mommy and I have not talked about that yet. For now, let's just think about Mother's Day."

"Okay." I drew in a deep breath and let it out slowly. "Mother's Day."

"How about if you and Andrew spend Saturday afternoon at the little house?" suggested Daddy. "You can celebrate with Mommy then. On Sunday you can join us in our celebration for Elizabeth and Nannie here."

"That sounds fine," I said.

"Good." Daddy smiled at me.

We went looking for Andrew then. We told him the news. Then Andrew and I worked on our go-cart some more.

No Chores,
No Allowance

Later in the afternoon, I was reading in my room. Andrew and I had grown tired of working on our go-cart. So we were taking a break. Andrew was playing with Sam. I was reading an old picture book called *Millions of Cats.*

"Hi, pumpkin," said Daddy. He knocked on my door. Then he sat on the edge of my bed.

"Hi," I replied.

"Are you feeling better about Mother's Day?"

"Much better."

"I want to be sure you really feel okay with our arrangements."

"I really do."

"Terrific," said Daddy. "I called Mommy and she sounded very happy to know she and Seth will see you next weekend." (I nodded.) "Now," Daddy went on, "I have an idea. Why don't you come outside with me?"

I jumped up. Then I took Daddy's hand and we walked outside together. This sounded mysterious — and exciting.

"What is it?" I asked.

Daddy led me to one of his flower gardens. It was the one he calls his English garden. It was bursting with plants that were either in bloom, or were going to bloom soon.

"Karen," said Daddy, "how would you like to help me take care of this garden?"

"Your *English* garden?" I replied. Daddy loves his gardens. He can be very picky about letting people help him with them.

"Sure," replied Daddy. "You are old enough. And you might like to have a nice, quiet place where you can come to think sometimes. A garden is good for that. A garden is peaceful. And beautiful."

"But how will I know what to do?" I asked.

"Oh, I will help you," replied Daddy. "You will not be on your own. I will show you what to do. Let's start with the rose-bushes."

Daddy and I were cutting the dead roses off the bushes when Elizabeth joined us in the garden. "Karen?" she said. (She did not look happy.)

"Yes?" I replied. (What I was thinking was Uh-oh.)

"I need to talk to you for a minute."

"Okay." I took off my gardening gloves. I sat beside Elizabeth on the lawn.

"Karen, do you remember our talk last night?"

I thought back to the night before. It seemed like a long time ago. "You mean

about doing chores?" I said finally.

"That's right. Karen, you did not make your bed again this morning. Your room is still a mess. And Charlie just separated the recycling things himself. He wanted to take them to the center, but you had not done your job."

"Oops," I said.

"So you will not be given your allowance this week. No chores, no allowance."

My mouth dropped open. "But I fed Emily Junior!" I exclaimed. "And — and right now I am helping Daddy in the garden."

"That is very nice, but helping your father in the garden is not one of your chores," said Elizabeth. "I asked you to do four things, and you have only done one of them — even after I gave you reminders."

I turned to my father. "Daddy!" I cried.

Daddy gave me a stern look. "Elizabeth is right," he said. "In this house when you do not do your chores, you do not get your allowance."

"THAT . . . IS . . . NOT . . . FAIR!" I yelled. I stomped out of the garden. I stomped across the lawn, through the house, and upstairs to my room. Then I made the bed and tidied up the mess.

Interrupting

On Sunday morning I remembered to make my bed. I picked up my clothes and put them away, too. I even straightened up my bookcase. When Elizabeth poked her head in my room, she said, "Very nice, Karen. Your room looks great."

I was tying a red ribbon in my hair. "Thanks," I replied.

Elizabeth took the ribbon out of my hands. "Here, let me do that for you. I will make a nice big bow."

"I do not want a big bow," I told her. "I

want the ribbons to hang down in back. I can do it. But thanks," I added.

"How about a pink ribbon, honey?" said Elizabeth. "Wouldn't pink look better with your shirt than red?"

"I like red."

"All right." Elizabeth left the room.

I was trying hard to be cheerful around Elizabeth. But I did not feel very cheerful. Elizabeth made too many suggestions. She was always telling me what to do, and how to do it, and what I should be wearing. Didn't she think I could do anything by myself? I am big enough to choose my clothes and to know what to eat or when to wear my glasses. Elizabeth made me feel as if nothing I did was good enough or quite right. I decided to have a little talk with myself. This is what I said:

"Karen, you were the one who asked for equal time at the big house and the little house. You were the one who said you wanted to spend more time with Daddy's family. So Mommy and Daddy and the lawyers figured out what to do. Now you better help make things work. You have to do your part. Be cheerful around Elizabeth."

Be cheerful, be cheerful, I repeated to myself.

And I thought Elizabeth was trying to be cheerful, too. She had not mentioned that I had lost my allowance. She did not seem angry. She did not make a big deal over what had happened. At lunchtime when I talked too loudly, she still smiled when she said, "Indoor voice, Karen." And when I talked too much, she still smiled when she said, "Give someone else a chance, honey."

But after lunch, when I tried to ask Elizabeth a question while she was on the telephone, she did not smile. She looked at me and frowned. She said crossly, "Not *now*, Karen. Can't you see I am *on* the *phone*?" Then she returned to her conversation.

Well, for heaven's sake.

I turned around. I flumped into the TV room. "Andrew," I said, "let's work on our go-cart some more."

Andrew followed me outside. We lugged the pieces of our go-cart to the driveway. Then we spread them out. We stood and looked at them.

"Well," I said.

"Well," said Andrew. "What do we do now?"

I was not sure. I tried to think about what real cars look like. Finally I said, "We will work on the part we sit in."

Andrew and I set to work. Soon Sam came by. "How are you going to steer your car?" he asked us. "Do you want some help?"

"No, thank you," we said.

Elizabeth came by. "My, look at this. Do you want some help?"

"No, thank you," we replied.

Andrew and I wanted to build the car ourselves. We did not want help. Especially not Elizabeth's.

Karen's Wicked
Stepmother

"Time to get up, kids," Elizabeth was calling.

I groaned. "Oh, no. Just five more minutes."

It was Monday morning. I like mornings. And I like school. But I did not feel like getting out of bed just then. I was too sleepy.

I lay in bed so long that I hardly had time to get dressed. I threw on a shirt and a skirt. Then I raced downstairs. Half of my big-house family was having breakfast in the kitchen. The other half had already eaten.

"Oh, my gosh! I'm late," I exclaimed. I grabbed a piece of toast as I sat down. "Nannie, I could hardly wake up," I said. "I had two funny dreams last night. I think that is why I am so sleepy. Those dreams kept me up. In one, I had just found this little kitten. But it looked more like — "

"Excuse me! Excuse me!" Andrew was raising his hand again.

"Just a minute, Andrew. This is a really great dream," I told him. "See, the kitten looked like a dog. Only somehow I knew it was just a kitten — "

"Nannie!" cried Emily Michelle.

"Wait, Emily," I said. "I am not finished. So I picked up the kitten and I was going to carry it around in my pocket."

"Excuse me," said Andrew again.

"*Wait*," I replied.

"Karen, *please* give them a chance to talk," said Elizabeth.

They did not have a single important

thing to say. All Andrew wanted to say was that he could not finish his breakfast. All Emily wanted to do was point to her cup and say, "See? Red."

Andrew and Emily are such babies.

After breakfast was over, I ran upstairs to brush my teeth. When I finished, Elizabeth said to me, "Karen, come here. I want to show you something." She led me toward my room.

"Elizabeth, I have to leave. I am going to be late," I said.

"Does that mean you are not going to be able to make your bed?" she asked.

I looked at my messy room. I sighed. I had already forgotten about my chores. "Can I do my chores after school?"

"You may," replied Elizabeth. "But if you keep forgetting to do them every morning, you will not get your allowance next weekend, either."

Boo and bullfrogs. I wanted to scream and stamp my foot. Instead, I said to myself, "Be cheerful, be cheerful."

I tried to smile at Elizabeth. "Okay," I said.

That morning, Mrs. Papadakis drove Hannie and Linny and me to school. While Linny and Mrs. Papadakis talked in the front seat, I complained to Hannie in the back seat.

"Elizabeth is so mean," I said. "She is always telling me how to do things. She thinks her ways are better. And she makes up too, too many rules. Do you know what? Everyone at the big house has to do chores. We have to do them *every day*. And if we don't, we do not get our allowance. And this is how many chores I have to do: four. Take care of Emily Junior, make my bed, keep my room neat, and put the recycling stuff in the bins."

"I have to do chores, too," said Hannie.

"Well, I bet your mother does not tell you to be quiet all the time. Elizabeth says I talk too much, and I talk too loudly. And I interrupt."

Mrs. Papadakis pulled up in front of the

school then. Hannie and I ran to our classroom to meet Nancy. The first thing I said to Nancy was, "Guess what. Elizabeth is awful. She makes up rules, and she is mean to me. Elizabeth is my wicked stepmother."

Losers

One day after school, Hannie and I were sitting on the curb in front of her house. It had rained that morning. Little rivers were running by our feet toward the sewer. Hannie picked up a green seed pod.

"Let's have races," she said. "You find a seed pod, too. Then we will put them in the water together. The one that goes down the sewer first wins."

"Okay," I replied.

Hannie won the first race.

"Best of three!" I cried. We held two

more races. (We had to find new seed pods each time.)

"Hi, you guys!" called Maria, as she and Bill and Melody stepped off their school bus.

The bus pulled away. Our friends joined us on the curb. Soon Timmy and Scott came by. Then Linny and David Michael and Andrew came outside.

"Well," said Bill. "My go-cart is almost finished."

"It *is*?" said David Michael.

"Yup," said Bill. "And you know what we should do today?"

"What?" asked Maria.

"Have a trial race. You know, a practice race."

"Yeah!" cried my friends.

"No!" I cried.

"Oh, Karen. Why not?" said David Michael crossly.

"Because the real race is more than two weeks away. Andrew and I have been working hard on our car, but it is not finished." I did not add that it was nowhere *near* finished. It had wheels, but that was about it. It was a box on wheels.

"Karen, *please* can we be in the race?" begged Andrew. "Everyone else is going to be in it. Please?" If there is anything Andrew wants it is to be just like the big kids, since he is littler than all of us.

"Yeah, come on, Karen," said Maria. "My car is not finished either."

"Neither is mine," said Hannie.

"Or mine," said Melody. "Nobody's is. Not even Bill's."

"Oh . . . all right," I finally agreed. But I had a bad feeling about the race. I just knew it was not a good idea.

My friends and I ran to our garages. We hauled out our go-carts. When we had gathered them on the sidewalk, I took a look at them. Bill had begun to paint his. It was blue, with orange flames on the sides. Hannie's had a seat with cushions. Scott's had a real steering wheel.

I glanced at the one Andrew and I were

making. It was a crate sitting on old wheels. I had not even thought about how to steer it.

"Who will judge our race?" Linny asked.

"Sam will," said David Michael. "I will go get him."

When Sam came outside, he helped my friends and me to line up our cars in the street. He watched for traffic. Then he ran to the bottom of the hill and shouted, "GO!"

We each took some running steps, pushing our go-carts, and then leaped into them. (Andrew was already in ours, and I stepped on his hand.) Our cars rolled down the hill. Since Andrew and I could not steer ours, it rolled into the curb. We did not even reach the bottom.

We lost the race. We came in last. (Melody won.)

Afterward, Sam said to Andrew and me, "Want some help?"

I knew he meant help building the cart. Sam is good at those things.

But I said, "No, thank you."

Later, Kristy offered us help, too. But I shook my head. David Michael was building his car by himself. Everyone was. So Andrew and I would, too.

The Fight

On Friday, Ms. Colman gave us home-work. We are not given much homework in second grade. But that day we each took a worksheet home. They were due on Mon-day. I wanted to finish mine before the weekend. So I sat down with it at the table in my bedroom.

Just before dinnertime, I was busy writ-ing prefix words when Elizabeth poked her head in my room. "Karen?" she said. "May I talk to you, please?"

"Sure," I replied. "You can sit down, um . . ." I looked at my bed. It was not made. And it was covered with papers and markers and books. I looked at my chair. It was covered with dirty clothes.

Elizabeth raised her eyebrows at me.

"Oops," I said.

"You have not made your bed once this week," said Elizabeth. She was standing in the doorway. Her arms were folded. "Your room is a mess. And do you know what Charlie is doing right now?" I shook my head. "He is doing his homework. What he *thought* he would be doing was taking our things to the recycling center. But he could not because you have not separated them. And this time he was not going to do it for you."

"Oh." I could not look at Elizabeth. I looked at the floor instead.

"Do you have anything to say for yourself?" asked Elizabeth.

I shook my head. "No."

"All right. Karen, I am very sorry but you will not get your allowance again this week. You have not earned it."

"But I wanted to buy a new book! And I owe Kristy fifty cents."

"I am sorry," said Elizabeth. She left the room.

I sat at my table for a moment longer. Then I left the room, too. I stomped down the hall, down the stairs, and out the back door. I stomped all the way to the flower garden. I looked around. I drew in a deep breath. Daddy was right. The garden is a peaceful place.

As I looked at the flowers, I got an idea. I should make a bouquet to take to Mommy the next day. Mommy would like a gift of flowers. Then I decided *not* to give Elizabeth the present I had made for her. She was too mean. Wicked stepmothers did not deserve cards and gifts. I wished I did not have to spend Sunday with Elizabeth. I wished I could spend the *real* Mother's Day with my *real* mother.

That was when I got my next idea. I ran out of the garden. I checked the driveway. Good. Daddy was home from work. I ran into the house. "Daddy!" I called.

"In the kitchen," he replied.

Daddy and Elizabeth were both in the kitchen. They were drinking iced tea. Elizabeth was probably telling him that I'd lost my allowance again.

I ignored Elizabeth. "Daddy," I said, "I want to spend the *real* Mother's Day with my *real* mother. I do not want to be with Elizabeth. Can I go to the little house instead?"

Daddy set his mouth in a line. "Absolutely not. And apologize to Elizabeth right now for being so rude. You hurt her feelings."

"But I want to be with Mommy."

"You will see her tomorrow. Karen, if you had asked me about this in some other way, I might have changed the plans. But you were deliberately cruel to Elizabeth just now. So I will not change the plans. Tell Elizabeth you are sorry."

"Sorry," I said. (I did not mean it.) I stomped away.

At bedtime, Elizabeth came to my room as usual. I glared at her. "I do not care to hear any more about Hoover," I told her.

Mother's Day at the Little House

On Saturday morning, I woke up feeling both mad and glad. I was still mad at Elizabeth about my allowance. But I was glad because Andrew and I were going to see Mommy and Seth that day.

After breakfast I gathered up my things for Mommy. I had made her a card and a present. Then I said to Daddy, "May I please pick a bouquet of flowers from the garden?"

Daddy nodded. "One bouquet," he replied.

I was careful with the bouquet. I picked only the flowers I really needed. (I do not think flowers like to be cut.)

Later that morning, Charlie drove Andrew and me to the little house. We ran inside with our flowers and cards and presents. We had not been there for almost two weeks.

"Here you are!" exclaimed Mommy. She threw her arms around us. She hugged Andrew and me at the same time.

"Happy Mother's Day!" we said.

"Thank you," replied Mommy. She held us away from her so she could look at us. She was crying a little.

"What is the matter?" asked Andrew.

I nudged him. "Nothing is the matter. She is happy."

Andrew shrugged.

I handed Mommy the flowers then. She cried some more.

"Open your presents now!" said Andrew. He thrust his at her. I held mine out, too. We could not wait a moment longer.

66

Seth laughed. "Slow down, you two," he said. "I will fix us something to drink. Then we can sit on the porch while your mom opens her gifts. Let's have a nice relaxing day."

So we did. Especially after Mommy stopped crying. Each of the presents and cards made her cry. But after that she was okay. We ate lunch in a restaurant. Then we went to the playground.

Later, when we were just sitting around the little house, I said to Mommy, "Elizabeth is a pain. She makes too many rules."

"Really?" replied Mommy.

I nodded. I did not tell her that I was the only one who had trouble remembering the rules. But I did say, "So I want to spend tomorrow, the real Mother's Day, here with you. And — and, um, I have permission," I said suddenly. "Daddy said I could."

"Did he?" exclaimed Mommy. "Oh, honey, that's wonderful!"

"So can you pick me up tomorrow morning?" I asked her.

"Well, of *course* I can. I will pick you up at ten-thirty."

"Perfect," I replied.

Andrew and Seth came in then. Andrew was talking about our go-cart. "It is a box on wheels," he was explaining. "It goes . . . well, not *fast*."

"It crawls along like a turtle," I spoke up. "And you cannot steer it."

"But we are not done with it," said Andrew.

"Would you like a little help?" asked Seth.

"Nope," I replied. Then I remembered to say, "Thank you."

"We are going to build it ourselves," added Andrew.

Seth looked at his watch then. "I hate to say so, kids, but it is about time for you to leave. Come on. Get ready to hop in the car."

Mommy did not want to drive with us back to Daddy's house. She let Seth drive us. We said our good-byes in the living room. Mommy put her arms around first Andrew, then me. We hugged and hugged. Just before we let go of each other Mommy said to me softly, "See you tomorrow morning, sweetie."

Karen Causes Trouble

When I woke up on Sunday morning, the big house was a busy place. Busier than usual.

It was Mother's Day.

Everyone was up and doing things. Well, except for Nannie and Elizabeth. They were awake. But Daddy was saying to them, "No, no, no. You may not get out of bed. You must stay there. That is an order."

Downstairs, Charlie and Andrew were fixing the special Mother's Day breakfasts. Charlie was cooking. Andrew was setting things on two trays. He even put roses from the garden into little bud vases.

When Charlie finally finished cooking, he and Andrew looked at the trays. "Fit for queens," said Charlie. He and Andrew carried the trays upstairs.

As soon as they left the kitchen, Kristy and Sam started working on lunch. (Daddy and Emily had already baked the merry-go-round cake.) David Michael was helping Emily color a picture for Nannie.

What was I doing? I sat grumpily in front of the TV set. I had not said, "Happy Mother's Day," to Elizabeth. (I had not even seen her.) At ten-thirty I heard a horn honk in the driveway. I leaped to my feet. That was Mommy. I had not told Daddy that I was going back to the little house. But I did not see what he could do about it, now that Mommy had arrived.

I raced to the front door and looked outside. Guess what. Daddy was already in the driveway. He was talking to Mommy.

I could hear what they were saying. And they sounded cross.

"Karen is going to spend the day with *you*?" (That was Daddy.) "She was just there yesterday."

"But she wanted to come again."

"Well, she can't."

"She said she had permission."

Daddy and Mommy both looked toward the house then. When they saw me at the door, they called me outside. Before they said a word, I knew I was in trouble. Again. I was probably in Big Trouble.

Sure enough. Mommy said, "Karen, you *lied*."

And Daddy said, "You disappointed your mother. And you have hurt Elizabeth's feelings again. Nannie's too."

Mommy's eyes had filled with tears. But her voice was very firm when she said, "You will have to be punished, Karen."

Daddy turned to me. "Honestly, Karen. How could you do this? What were you

thinking? Besides, I thought you wanted to spend more time here."

I looked at my feet. I felt miserable. "I did," I said. "I mean, I do."

Daddy and Mommy sighed.

"Look," said Mommy finally. "We had our Mother's Day celebration yesterday. And it was very nice. Today is the celebration for Nannie and Elizabeth. I don't want you to spoil it for them, Karen."

I shuffled my feet. I did not say whether I would spoil it. "What is my punishment going to be?" I asked.

Mommy and Daddy looked at each other. Even though they are divorced, they can still talk with their eyes.

"We will discuss it tonight," Daddy told me. "Right now, there is too much to do. And I'm sure your mother wants to get home. Go inside now, Karen."

I stomped to the front door. Mommy and Daddy were still talking. When I closed the door a moment later, I heard Mommy's car pull away.

Andrew met me in the front hallway. "Hey, was that Mommy?" he asked. "What was she doing here?"

"Nothing," I replied. I went right on stomping. I did not stop until I was in my room. Then I slammed the door behind me. I threw myself on my bed. (The bed was not made.) I did not plan to come out.

Mother's Day at
the Big House

Guess what. I had to leave my room after all. David Michael made me. He knocked on my door and would not stop.

"I know you are in there," he said. "I can smell you."

"You cannot!" I yelled.

"See, you are in there. Now come out. We are in charge of the show, and we need to have a rehearsal."

Finally I came out, just so David Michael would stop yelling. But I was not much help during the rehearsal. When everyone else was singing, I hummed the tune to "Greasy Grimy Gopher Guts."

I had made a decision. I was going to ruin Mother's Day for Elizabeth.

I think I did a pretty good job.

Elizabeth and Nannie had finished their breakfasts in bed. Now they were dressed (in their most comfortable clothes). And they were sitting in the living room waiting for the show to begin.

My brothers and sisters and I filed into the room. We lined up. They sang. I folded my arms and clamped my mouth shut. (Daddy glared at me, but he did not say anything.)

Presents came next. I ran to my room and got Nannie's present. (I left Elizabeth's in the closet.) Later, I gave Nannie her card and gift. I gave Elizabeth a bouquet of dead roses from the garden.

"You are in mighty big trouble, young lady," Daddy whispered to me.

I did eat lunch with everybody, but afterward, when Daddy brought out the merry-go-round cake, and we crowded around Elizabeth and Nannie, I turned my back.

"You are really going to get it," David Michael said to me.

Even Kristy nudged me in the side and said, "You are being an enormous brat, Karen." She looked awfully cross.

By then, I did not know how to stop what I had started. I knew I was hurting Elizabeth (Nannie, too). I was beginning to feel like a wicked stepdaughter. But I was a snowball rolling down a hill. I could not stop.

Soon Daddy said, "Let's take a family picture. I will get the camera with the timer."

Daddy posed us in the backyard. "Karen, you stand here," he said.

I jerked away. "Not next to Elizabeth."

"Karen," said Daddy.

But Elizabeth stepped in. "After the picture it will be time for a talk, Karen."

Getting Along

Flash! went Daddy's camera.

I was standing apart from my family. I was scowling.

"Okay, Karen," said Elizabeth. She took my hand. "Let's take a walk. We need to discuss a few things. Right now."

Elizabeth led me out of the backyard. We started down the street. I was pretty sure I was in Very Big Trouble. But guess what. When Elizabeth began talking, she did not sound angry at all.

"Karen," she said, "I think the new custody arrangements have been more of a change than anyone realized they would be. And they have been a change for everyone. Not just for you and Andrew, but for your mom and dad and Seth and Nannie and me, as well. And for your brothers and sisters. We all have lots of things to adjust to. For one thing, I bet you miss your mom and Seth and the little house."

"I guess so," I admitted. "I did not think I would, but I do. I am still glad to be here, though. Andrew and I really *wanted* to spend more time here. But the big house sure is different from the little house. Andrew and I do not have chores at the little house. I mean, we help out. But we do not have *assigned* chores. We just do things when Mommy or Seth asks us to."

Elizabeth nodded. "That is true," she agreed. "The two houses are different. But living at two houses — equal time — means living with two sets of rules. When you are here at the big house you have to live by the same set of rules as the other kids here.

And you will be treated just like the other kids. Same rules, same privileges. Would you really *want* to be treated differently? If you were, you would not feel as much a part of the family. You would feel as if you did not belong. Two sets of rules might be confusing, but it is the only way to work things."

I sighed. "It is really just part of being a two-two."

Elizabeth smiled. "Do you know what, Karen? I should explain something to you that I probably should have explained before. There is a reason for the rules and the assigned chores at the big house. It is because the big house *is* a big house — with a big family living in it. Keeping track of ten people, and running a household for them, is not easy. It takes planning and organization. Otherwise, this place would be a mess! But if everyone pitches in, we can keep it running smoothly. The little house is probably easier to run. So, here at the big house, everyone does chores. If they don't, they lose their allowances. Kristy and her brothers know this, Andrew and Emily are learning it, and you have to learn it, too."

I nodded. "Okay."

"Now," Elizabeth went on, "maybe I did not make this clear at the beginning. If I did not, it was because I wanted you and Andrew to feel comfortable here. I didn't want to overwhelm you. Anyway, now that you understand about the chores, what other things do we need to talk about?"

"We-ell . . ." I tried to think of a nice way to say what I wanted to say. "Elizabeth, you make too many suggestions. You are always suggesting different ways to do things. *Your* ways. I feel like I do not do *any*thing right."

"Fair enough," said Elizabeth. "I will stop making so many suggestions. If you will stop talking so much. And stop interrupting me when I'm on the phone."

That sounded like a fair deal. So I agreed to it. Then I agreed to one more deal. Elizabeth and Nannie would remind me every day to do my chores. And I would do them without complaining.

Elizabeth and I turned and headed back to the big house. On the way, I said, "Elizabeth? Will you tell me some more about Hoover tonight?"

And Elizabeth replied, "I would be happy to."

Grease

During the next two weeks, Elizabeth and I tried very hard to get along. We stuck to our deals, and that helped. Elizabeth only made suggestions that were *really* necessary. Like the one she made the day I ran out the door on my way to Hannie's so her dad could drive us to school. As I ran by Elizabeth she said, "May I make a suggestion, Karen?"

I looked at her warily. "What?"

"That you go back inside and get your lunch and your homework."

"Oh! Thanks, Elizabeth!"

And I tried not to talk so much, especially during meals. I let Andrew and Emily talk more. But once I *had* to interrupt Elizabeth when she was on the phone. I thought she would want to know that whatever was in the microwave had just exploded. And she did.

Also, every morning, Elizabeth poked her head in my room and said, "Time to get up, honey. Make your bed and tidy up your room before you come downstairs."

Every afternoon, as soon as I came home from school, Nannie would point to the recycling stuff and say, "Remember your job, Karen."

I found that if I separated the stuff once a day, it only took a few minutes. And Charlie was much more pleasant about going to the recycling center. Sometimes he even let me ride along in the Junk Bucket with him. I had not missed my allowance again.

Meanwhile, Andrew and I worked on our

go-cart. Guess what. It was actually beginning to look more like a go-cart. We were working hard. I did not want us to be embarrassed during the race. So we made the box more sturdy. Also, I figured out a way to steer our car. I took a good look at that old red wagon to see how it steered. Then I tried to make our car steer the same way. It did not steer nearly as well, but it steered. At least we would not sail into the crowd of people watching the race. We would be able to stay on the road. And I had worked on the wheels to make our car faster. In fact, it could really zoom along. Nannie watched Andrew take a ride in it one day, and afterward she told both of us we would have to start wearing crash helmets. I was flattered. (Andrew was disappointed about the lampshade, though.)

On a Thursday, four days before our race, Andrew and I decided our car was finished. We took it for another run down the hill. Elizabeth was just coming home from work, and she watched us zoom past her. She was waiting for us in the driveway when we dragged the car back.

"That is really something," said Elizabeth. "It's a speed demon."

"It still does not steer very well, though," I replied.

Andrew and I stood in the driveway. We looked at Elizabeth. She looked back at us. I was waiting for her to make a suggestion. I could tell she was not going to, though. I could not blame her. Finally I said, "Well, what do you think? About the steering?"

"Hmm. Have you tried grease?"

"Grease? No, we greased the wheels, though. And they are much faster. Maybe we should grease all the steering stuff, too."

So we did. Then we took the car out again. Elizabeth watched us roll away. Now our car shot down the hill, *and* it was easy to steer.

"Cool!" cried Andrew as he climbed out of the box.

"Hey, I have an idea," I said. "I hope we can find some paint in the garage."

We found several cans. We painted our car blue. Then we painted the words SPEED DEMON on each side of the box. We painted them in red, and then we outlined them in white so they would show up better. I *almost* asked Kristy to help with the outlining. Then I did it by myself.

The go-cart was finished. Andrew and I were proud of it. We had built it by ourselves, with only one intsy little suggestion from Elizabeth.

The Race

After we had painted the go-cart, I had a little problem. It was Andrew. He kept looking at our beautiful racing car and saying, "Now we are going to win!"

"Andrew, our car looks great," I agreed. "But that does not mean we are going to win. The other cars look great, too."

That was the truth. In fact, most of the cars looked a lot better than ours. David Michael's was one of them. He had found some very cool stuff in the lot where the house was being built. Then, on Saturday,

Andrew and I watched him take his car for a test run. Elizabeth and Sam and Kristy watched, too. David Michael zoomed down that hill. He went so fast his hair blew out behind him.

"Is he faster than us?" Andrew asked me.

"I'm not sure," I replied.

Elizabeth thought he was fast, too. "Wear a helmet from now on," she told him. "Andrew and Karen are also wearing them."

David Michael looked cross.

"Want to borrow the lampshade?" Andrew asked him.

On Sunday, Bill, Timmy, and Maria took their finished cars on test runs. They looked awfully fast, too.

"But no one is faster than us," said Andrew.

"Andrew. Do not expect to win," I told him. "I mean it. Those cars are faster and better than ours. But at least when we race tomorrow we will probably not come in last. And we will not ride into the curb. Just have fun tomorrow, Andrew."

* * *

Finally Monday arrived. It was the day of the race. It was also our last full day at the big house. On Tuesday, Andrew and I would go back to Mommy's after school. I could not believe the month was almost over.

My friends and I had decided to hold the race at three o'clock in the afternoon. By quarter of three, people were lining the street along the hill. They were the parents and grandparents and brothers and sisters and friends of the ten kids in the race.

"Ooh, look at our audience," I whispered to Hannie. We were lining up our cars in the street. I noticed that all of us kids were wearing helmets now.

Sam was going to start the race. He waited until my friends and I were standing ready behind our cars. Then he aimed a water pistol into the sky. (The pistol was shaped like a bunny.) "On your marks!" yelled Sam. "Get set! GO!" He shot a stream of water over his head.

My friends and I each took five running steps, pushing our cars. Then we leaped into them. I stepped on Andrew's hand again. But he did not seem to notice.

"Karen, we are flying!" he cried.

Well, of course we were not really flying, but we felt as if we were.

Zoom! We passed Hannie's car. Zoom! We passed David Michael's car! Zoom! We passed Maria's and Timmy's and Linny's. We almost rode into Melody's, but I jerked our car away.

The next thing I knew, Andrew and I were sailing across the finish line. Bill Korman was right beside us. As soon as Charlie had helped us to stop, I said, "See, Andrew? We did not come in last."

Charlie looked at me strangely. "Did not come in last?" he said. "Karen, you and Andrew came in first. You won the race!"

My mouth dropped open. I could not believe it. We had won. Bill had come in second. Andrew and I had beaten the oldest kid in the race.

Happy Mother's Day!

My big-house family held a barbecue that night. We were celebrating Memorial Day and the go-cart race and the end of Andrew's and my first month at the big house.

"The next time you are here," said Kristy as we were setting the picnic tables in the backyard, "it will be July. Maybe we will have another barbecue for the Fourth of July."

"Cool," I said.

"Are you happy to be going to your mom's house tomorrow?"

I thought for a moment. "Happy and sad," I said finally. "This month started out to be . . . not so great. But then it turned out to be fine."

Elizabeth had decided on a vegetable barbecue. So this is what we grilled: veggie shish kebabs and corn on the cob. Also, we made a huge salad full of all kinds of vegetables.

My big-house family sat at the picnic tables and ate from plastic plates. (Andrew had wanted to use paper, but Charlie said they were wasteful.) As we ate, the sky grew darker and the first fireflies came out. We watched them wink on and off.

"When I was little," said Kristy, "I used to think that if you filled an entire jar with fireflies, you could use it as a flashlight."

"Can't you?" replied Andrew.

Kristy smiled. "Well, maybe we will try it later this summer."

"Karen?" said David Michael, who was sitting next to me. "When you leave tomorrow, are you going to take the Speed Demon?"

"I do not think so," I said. "It is too big. We will probably leave it here."

"Well, while you are gone, could I look at it? I want to see how you made it steer. Maybe I can make my car work better." David Michael had come in fourth in the race. He did not seem to mind.

"Sure," I replied.

"You can have the lampshade, too," offered Andrew.

Emily Michelle started to get fussy then, so Nannie took her inside. The rest of us cleared the tables. We carried the things into the kitchen, but then I went back outdoors by myself. I stood in the yard. I breathed in the springtime smells. The air had become chilly, but I could feel summer in it.

I thought about the past month. I thought about Elizabeth and rules and go-carts and flower gardens. And then I thought of a good idea. I found Daddy's shears. I carried them carefully to the garden. I cut a bouquet of flowers. Then I returned the shears to the garage, and brought the flowers inside.

"Elizabeth?" I called. (I remembered to use my indoor voice.)

"What is it, honey?" Elizabeth was leaving Emily's room. She had just put her to bed.

I held the flowers out. "Happy Mother's Day," I said softly. I was hoping the bouquet would make up for the dead flowers I had given her when I was feeling so angry.

"Oh, Karen," said Elizabeth. "Thank you." Her eyes filled with tears. (I really don't understand why grownups cry when they are happy. Maybe when I am a grownup myself I will understand.)

"You're welcome," I replied. Elizabeth gave me a hug. Then I said, "Are you going to finish the story about Hoover tonight?"

"As soon as you are ready for bed. And Karen, thank you for doing your chores these last two weeks. Will you remember to do them when you come back?"

"I hope so," I said. "I will try very hard."

"That is all I can ask for."

I went to my room then to get ready for my last night at the big house.

About the Author

ANN M. MARTIN lives in New York City and loves animals, especially cats. She has two cats of her own, Mouse and Rosie.

Other books by Ann M. Martin that you might enjoy are *Stage Fright*; *Me and Katie (the Pest)*; and the books in *The Baby-sitters Club* series.

Ann likes ice cream and *I Love Lucy*. And she has her own little sister, whose name is Jane.

BABY-SITTERS
Little Sister

Don't miss #50

KAREN'S LUCKY PENNY

"Could we go to Funland this summer? With the Gianellis and Nancy's family and Kathryn's family? And could we bring Hannie with us?" I told them what my friends and I had been talking about that afternoon.

Mommy and Seth did not say no and they did not say yes. They did say, "Do you know what the admission charge for Funland is?"

"No," said Andrew and I.

"It is forty dollars for adults and twenty-five dollars for kids under twelve."

"Forty dollars?" I repeated. "Oh, no. We will never get to go!"

"Well, let us think about it," said Mommy.

"Really?"

"Really."

LITTLE 🍎 APPLE

BABY-SITTERS
Little Sister™

by Ann M. Martin, author of *The Baby-sitters Club*®

❑	MQ44300-3	#1	Karen's Witch	$2.95
❑	MQ44259-7	#2	Karen's Roller Skates	$2.95
❑	MQ44299-7	#3	Karen's Worst Day	$2.95
❑	MQ44264-3	#4	Karen's Kittycat Club	$2.95
❑	MQ44258-9	#5	Karen's School Picture	$2.95
❑	MQ44298-8	#6	Karen's Little Sister	$2.95
❑	MQ44257-0	#7	Karen's Birthday	$2.95
❑	MQ42670-2	#8	Karen's Haircut	$2.95
❑	MQ43652-X	#9	Karen's Sleepover	$2.95
❑	MQ43651-1	#10	Karen's Grandmothers	$2.95
❑	MQ43650-3	#11	Karen's Prize	$2.95
❑	MQ43649-X	#12	Karen's Ghost	$2.95
❑	MQ43648-1	#13	Karen's Surprise	$2.75
❑	MQ43646-5	#14	Karen's New Year	$2.75
❑	MQ43645-7	#15	Karen's in Love	$2.75
❑	MQ43644-9	#16	Karen's Goldfish	$2.75
❑	MQ43643-0	#17	Karen's Brothers	$2.75
❑	MQ43642-2	#18	Karen's Home-Run	$2.75
❑	MQ43641-4	#19	Karen's Good-Bye	$2.95
❑	MQ44823-4	#20	Karen's Carnival	$2.75
❑	MQ44824-2	#21	Karen's New Teacher	$2.95
❑	MQ44833-1	#22	Karen's Little Witch	$2.95
❑	MQ44832-3	#23	Karen's Doll	$2.95
❑	MQ44859-5	#24	Karen's School Trip	$2.95
❑	MQ44831-5	#25	Karen's Pen Pal	$2.95
❑	MQ44830-7	#26	Karen's Ducklings	$2.75
❑	MQ44829-3	#27	Karen's Big Joke	$2.95
❑	MQ44828-5	#28	Karen's Tea Party	$2.95

More Titles... ➡

Now THE BABY-SITTERS CLUB®

★ is a Video Club too!